D0561176

MAGIC LEMONADE

Other titles in the bunch:

Big Dog and Little Dog Go Sailing
Big Dog and Little Dog Visit the Moon
Colin and the Curly Claw
Dexter's Journey
Follow the Swallow
"Here I Am!" said Smedley

Horrible Haircut
Magic Lemonade
The Magnificent Mummies
Midnight in Memphis
Peg
Shoot!

Crabtree Publishing Company
www.crabtreebooks.com

PMB 16A, 350 Fifth Avenue
Suite 3308
New York, NY 10118

612 Welland Avenue
St. Catharines, Ontario
Canada, L2M 5V6

Dunbar, Joyce.
    Magic lemonade / Joyce Dunbar ; illustrated by Jan McCafferty.
      p. cm. -- (Blue Bananas)
    Summary: Bossy Zoe pretends she is a queen, but her friends
ignore her until she offers them magic lemonade.
    ISBN 0-7787-0839-X -- ISBN 0-7787-0885-3 (pbk.)
    [1. Bossiness--Fiction. 2. Kings, queens, rulers, etc.--Fiction. 3.
Lemonade--Fiction. 4. Humorous stories.] I. McCafferty, Jan, ill. II.
Title. III. Series
    PZ7.D8944 Mae 2002
    [E]--dc21
                                        2001032437
                                            LC

Published by Crabtree Publishing in 2002
First published in 2001 by Egmont Children's Books Limited
Text copyright © Joyce Dunbar 2001
Illustrations copyright © Jan McCafferty 2001
The author and illustrator have asserted their moral rights
Paperback ISBN 0-7787-0885-3
Reinforced Hardcover Binding ISBN 0-7787-0839-X

1 2 3 4 5 6 7 8 9 0 Printed in Italy 0 9 8 7 6 5 4 3 2 1

MAGIC LEMONADE

Mishawaka-Penn-Harris
Public Library
Mishawaka, Indiana

Written by
Joyce Dunbar

Illustrated by
Jan McCafferty

Blue Bananas

For Madeline,
Edward and Grace
J.D.

For Andy
love J.M.

Zoe tottered into the yard. She was wearing high heels.

"Today I am a queen," she announced.

"How can you be a queen? You are not dressed like a queen," said Sam.

Zoe took a tablecloth from the clothesline. She took some clothespins too.

She wrapped the tablecloth around herself and pinned it with the clothespins.

6

"There! Now I am dressed like a queen,"
said Zoe.

"How can you be a queen? You do not
have a crown like a queen," said Joe.

7

"I do have a crown," said Zoe. "I forgot to put it on. Dee! Will you pass me the pin bag!"

Her Majesty awaits!

8

Dee passed the pin bag to Zoe.

"You make a silly queen," laughed Sam.

Zoe took some pins out of the pin bag.

She took two white pins, three blue pins,

and five pink pins.

She pinned them on to her headband.

"There! Now I have a crown!" said Zoe.

Perfect!

"And I am not a silly queen. I am a
splendid queen."

11

"You are not a queen. You do not have a throne to sit on," said Joe.

"I do have a throne," said Zoe. "But it is not a throne to sit on. It is a throne to stand on."

Her Majesty wins again.

13

She climbed onto the wooden steps. Her tablecloth gown hung down to the ground. Her crown of clothespins reached high.

"There!" said Zoe. "I am a tall and stately queen on my throne! You must all do as I say!"

Oh, for a pair of wings!

As usual!

"We don't want to play queens," said
Joe. "We are going on a snail hunt
with Todd."
"Good," said Zoe. "I order you to go on
a snail hunt!"

"Then we won't go on a snail hunt," said Sam. "We will play conga-bonga instead."

"Good!" said Zoe. "I order you to play conga-bonga instead. The queen will come to visit."

"Then we won't play conga-bonga," said Joe. Joe and Sam and Dee started to walk away.

"I banish you from my kingdom," said Zoe.

"We were going anyway!" said Joe.

Zoe climbed down from the wooden steps and tottered over to the old water pump. She pumped the handle up and down.

"Come on down!" shouted Zoe. "Get
your magic lemonade here!"

Joe and Sam and Dee came back.

"What magic lemonade?" asked Sam.

"Magic lemonade from the magic

lemonade pump," said Zoe.

"That isn't a magic lemonade pump," said Dee. "That's an old water pump and it doesn't even have any water."

"Maybe not," said Zoe. "But when a queen pumps the handle, magic lemonade comes out."

"Where?" said Sam.

Zoe pumped the handle again.

"There!" said Zoe. "Magic lemonade!"
She cupped her hands under the pump
and tasted some.

"Mmmm! Delicious!"

"There is no lemonade! There isn't
anything at all," said Sam.

Nothing!

26

"Can't you see the magic lemonade?" said Zoe. "Can't you hear the lemonade splashing? Can't you taste the magic lemonade?"

Mmmm, delicious!

"There is no lemonade," said Sam.

It fizzes!

"That's because you don't believe I'm a queen," said Zoe. "If you believed that I really was a queen, you would hear the magic lemonade . . .

. . . you would see the magic lemonade.

It sparkles!

You would taste the magic lemonade.

You could all have a drink of the magic

lemonade."

Joe and Sam and Dee licked their lips.

Zoe was making them thirsty.

"But first, you've got to believe I'm a

queen," said Zoe.

Every inch
a queen.

"All right, we believe you," said Dee.

"Really, really?" said Zoe.

"Really, really," said Dee.

"Say 'Your Majesty'," said Zoe.

"Your Majesty," said Dee and Sam and Joe.

"Bow to the queen," said Zoe.

Joe and Sam and Dee bowed to the queen.

"Now for the magic lemonade," said Zoe.

She pumped the handle again.

There was nothing, nothing at all.

"Oh dear," said Zoe. "No more magic lemonade. I must have used it all up.

What a good idea!

Never mind. I am a very kind queen. I am sure there is a jug of magic lemonade in the fridge at home. I will go and get it."

"Make way for the queen!"

They all made way for the queen. Zoe
swept past them.

"You must all bring something to eat. That is my royal command. We will have a royal feast in the royal pavilion!"

Zoe tottered off home. "She's not a queen at all," grumbled Dee. "She's a bossy boots."

All the same Dee did as Zoe said.

"What a showoff," muttered Joe.

All the same, he did as he was told.

"She always wants to be IT," complained

Sam, and went looking for something to eat.

Zoe returned with some magic lemonade. Joe brought raisins. Dee had cookies. Sam had bananas. They had a wonderful feast in the royal kitchen.

Hip-hip!

"Three cheers for Queen Bossy Boots,"

said Dee.

"Three cheers for Her Royal Showoff,"

said Joe.

"Three cheers for IT!" said Sam.

"I am not a bossy boots," said Zoe

taking off her cloak.

"I am not Her Royal Showoff," she

added, taking off her crown.

"I am not IT," she said, kicking off her

high heel shoes.

"I am not a queen either," she said,

ruffling her hair into a tangled mess.

"Now I am a magician! That is not magic lemonade. That is magic potion. It will turn you all into . . .

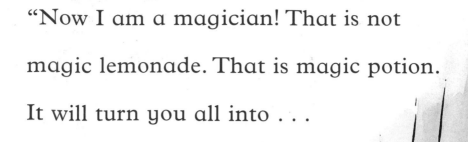

. . . FROGS!"